GRANDMA
LIVES IN A PERFUME VILLAGE

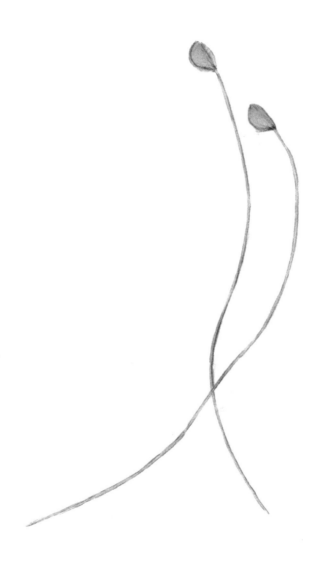

Praise for *Grandma Lives in a Perfume Village*

"... a tender look at the time just before a child understands the finality of death.
Danowski's realistic illustrations ... add a wistful, vintage-photo feel." —*New York Times Book Review*

"The beautifully rendered watercolor illustrations are warm,
realistic, and deeply human." —*School Library Journal*

A Batchelder Honor Book

First published in the United States, Great Britain, Canada, Australia, and New Zealand in 2015
by NorthSouth Books Inc., an imprint of NordSüd Verlag AG, CH-8005 Zürich, Switzerland.
Distributed in the United States by NorthSouth Books Inc., New York 10016.

Library of Congress Cataloging-in-Publication Data is available.
Printed in Latvia by Livonia Print, Riga, May 2016.
ISBN: 978-0-7358-4216-8
3 5 7 9 · 10 8 6 4 2
www.northsouth.com

GRANDMA
LIVES IN A PERFUME VILLAGE

FANG SUZHEN

SONJA DANOWSKI

Translated by Huang Xiumin

North South

Xiao Le's* grandma lived in the faraway Perfume Village.
It had been a long time since he saw her.

*The name Xiao Le is pronounced Shall La and means "little joy".

Then one morning his mom said, "It's time for us to visit Grandma."

Putting a small backpack on his shoulders, Xiao Le said happily, "Great, I can ride the train again. I will bring my truck to show Grandma."

It was a long train ride, but finally they arrived at Grandma's house. Xiao Le jumped to press the doorbell. But it wasn't Grandma who answered the door.

"This is Grandma's neighbor. Say hello to Aunt Zhou!" Xiao Le's mom said.

"Hurry in! Your grandma is not feeling well. She's in bed," said Aunt Zhou.

Xiao Le followed his mom into Grandma's room, clinging to her dress. Grandma was lying in bed, looking much older than in the photo of her at home! Xiao Le hid behind his mom's back.

She asked him, "Didn't you want to show Grandma your truck?"

Xiao Le just held the truck more tightly!

"You've come at the right moment," said Aunt Zhou. "I'll go home and will come back in a little while."

Xiao Le's mom said to him, "Stay here and look after Grandma while I make some snacks, okay?"

Xiao Le stood at the door, hugging the truck and looking at Grandma from afar.

Cough, cough! Grandma said, "Water . . . water . . ."

Xiao Le ran to his mom and said, "Grandma wants some water."

His mom came in, helped Grandma take a drink, and smoothed her quilt.

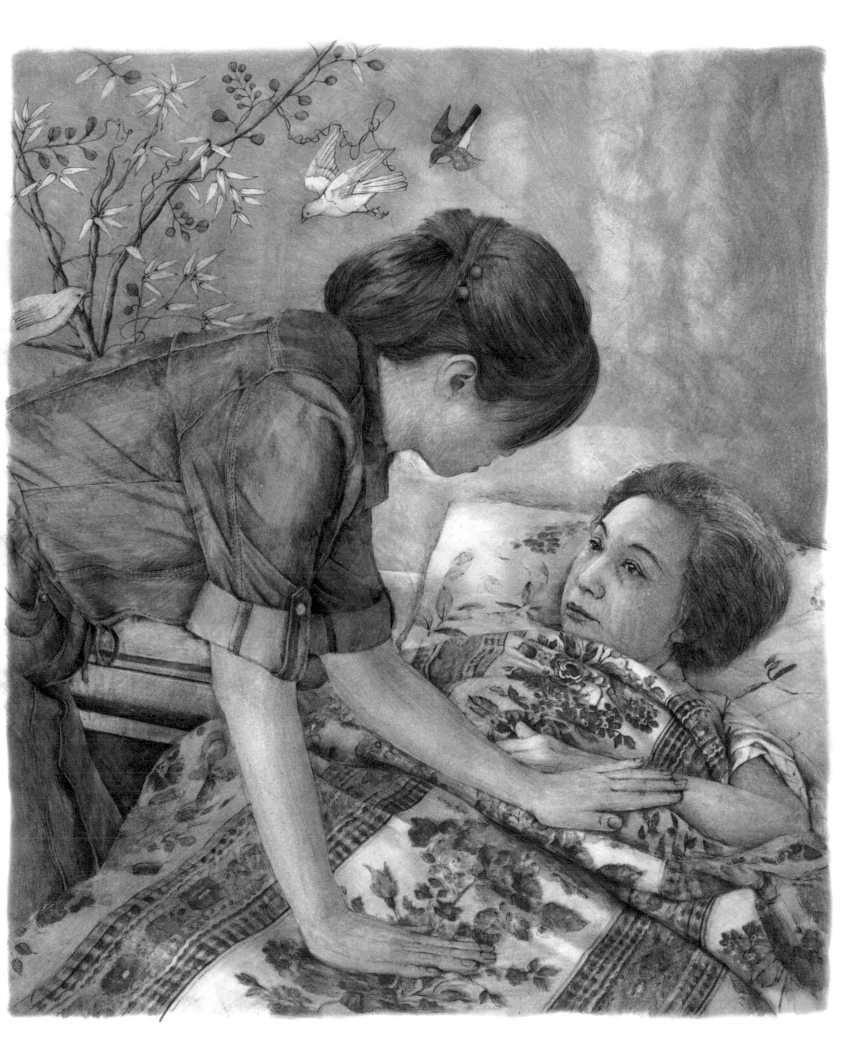

A moment later Grandma started to toss and turn. Worried that Grandma might fall off the bed, Xiao Le nervously called his mom, "Grandma is moving around!"

Mom touched Grandma's forehead and said, "Grandma has to take some medicine. Won't you help her?"

Xiao Le carefully placed the pills in Grandma's mouth, one by one.

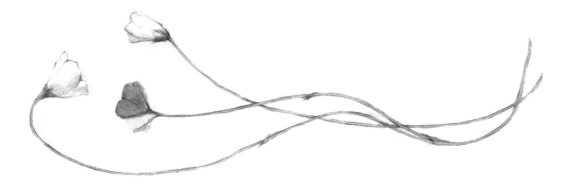

With Grandma resting comfortably, Mom went outside to wash her mom's clothes. Xiao Le seated himself on a stool, still not daring to go near.

A black cat silently jumped onto the bed.

Grandma beckoned. "Xiao Le, come and pet Shadow. She's gentle and won't bite you."

Xiao Le slowly moved closer and touched Shadow.

Meow! Shadow mewed.

Xiao Le touched her again, and Grandma gently patted Xiao Le on the head.

Xiao Le looked at the large photo next to Grandma's bed.

Grandma smiled and said, "That is your grandpa and your mother. This photo was taken many years ago.

"Your mom was a good child. She once stayed in the bathroom for a long time. When I opened the door, I found her cleaning the potty-chair. . . ."

Xiao Le burst out, "I can clean the potty-chair, too!"

Grandma grinned; her dry lips cracked.

The sun was casting its light softly through the curtain.

Grandma said in a husky voice, "I'd like to sit in the sun. Give me your hand, dear boy."

Mom was hanging clothes in the yard.

Grandma pointed at a large meadow of wood sorrel and said, "When your mother was a little girl, she was fond of playing a game with me."

Grandma picked two plants of wood sorrel, twined them together, and explained to Xiao Le, "Hold this end and I'll hold the other. The one whose wood sorrel breaks first is the loser. Your mother cried every time she lost."

The game began. Xiao Le and Grandma pulled back and forth. Each time Xiao Le won, and he laughed with great delight!

Xiao Le asked Grandma to play the game with Mom. Grandma lost again, and Xiao Le asked, "You lose every time. Why don't you cry?"

Grandma pretended to cry, but then she said, "Xiao Le has come to see Grandma. I'm so happy that I don't want to cry."

The three of them had afternoon tea in the yard.

Xiao Le took a bite of biscuit and said, "I'm so happy!"

After sitting for a while, Grandma was not feeling well again and had to return to the room to lie in bed. Xiao Le smoothed the quilt for Grandma in the way his mom did, then took out his toy and said, "My truck will sleep with you, Grandma."

Grandma closed her eyes with a smile.

Xiao Le walked out of the room and saw his mom talking with Aunt Zhou. His mom was wiping tears from her eyes.

Xiao Le didn't know what had happened.

He could do nothing but sit down to watch TV.

When the moon rose, his mom said, "It's very late, and we should go back home."

Xiao Le picked up his backpack and said aloud, "Good-bye, Grandma! See you, Aunt Zhou!"

Grandma returned the truck to Xiao Le, took him by the hand,and said, "Xiao Le is a good boy! Come to visit Grandma again, okay?"

Aunt Zhou promised to take good care of Grandma. Then they hurried off to catch the last train.

From that day on Xiao Le never saw Grandma again.

His mom said, "Grandma has left Perfume Village and moved into heaven."

"Where in heaven?" asked Xiao Le.

"It might be another Perfume Village. Your grandma loved living there."

Xiao Le believed that the Perfume Village in heaven must be farther away and couldn't be reached by train, for his mom often stared into the sky while shedding tears. Xiao Le knew that his mom was missing her mom.

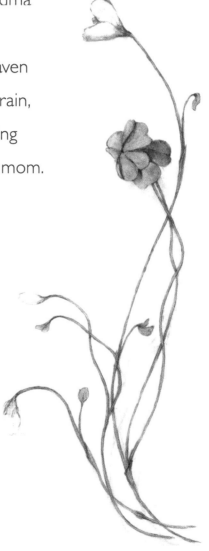

Xiao Le patted his mom on the shoulder and said, "Don't cry! Your mom has gone to heaven to drink afternoon tea with her mom. Grandma, do you have wood sorrel in heaven? Does anybody play games with you?"

Hearing his words, his mom held Xiao Le in her arms and shed more tears.

Day by day, Xiao Le couldn't remember how long Grandma had been away. However, whenever Xiao Le took a walk with his mom and saw the golden setting sun, a big smile would come onto his face.

"Look, Mom, Grandma is frying an egg in heaven!"

When the moon rose, Xiao Le would exclaim happily, "Look, Mom, Grandma has turned on the light! It's evening in heaven too."

One time when it rained and Xiao Le couldn't go out to play, he looked fretfully at the sky and said, "Grandma, don't wash your clothes! Water is dripping!"

This time his mom didn't weep but softly hugged Xiao Le and said, "I believe my mom has really moved into another Perfume Village. She washes dishes, does laundry, and drinks afternoon tea as usual, doesn't she?"

Xiao Le nodded heartily.

Then, all of a sudden, he thought of something very important, "Mom, don't go there to have afternoon tea with Grandma! Just stay here and drink tea with me, okay?"

His mom hugged him tightly and said gently, "The Perfume Village in heaven is too far away to be reached by train. . . ."

FANG SUZHEN is a seasoned children's author who emerged onto Taiwan's children's literary circle in 1975, engaging in and creating children's poetry, fairy tales, and picture books. In addition to her work as an author, Fang Suzhen also translates and edits language textbooks and volunteers her time storytelling. Through her many years of promoting reading in Hong Kong, Singapore, Malaysia, and beyond, she has become affectionately known, to young and old readers alike, as "Miss Rumphus, the woman who sows the seeds of reading."

Fang Suzhen has written more than two hundred books and has won numerous awards, including the Hongjian Quan Children's Literature Award, the Yanghuan Children's Award, the *Mandarin Daily News* Moody Award, and the United Daily News Group's Annual Award for best children's book.

SONJA DANOWSKI is a German artist and illustrator with a particular focus on how drawn images can help preserve human memory. Her work has been selected several times for the Illustrators Exhibition at the Bologna Children's Book Fair, and she has received numerous international awards for her art. In 2013, she was honored with a Gold Medal by the Korean Nami Island International Picture Book Illustration Concours, which led to this collaboration with the Chinese children´s book publisher CCPPG (China Children's Press & Publication Group). She lives in Berlin.